For daddy bears everywhere
A R

For Jeff, for your love and encouragement
A E

LITTLE TIGER PRESS
An imprint of Magi Publications
1 The Coda Centre, 189 Munster Road, London SW6 6AW
www.littletigerpress.com

First published in Great Britain 2007
This edition published in 2007

Text copyright © Alison Ritchie 2007
Illustrations copyright © Alison Edgson 2007
Alison Ritchie and Alison Edgson have asserted their rights
to be identified as the author and illustrator of this work
under the Copyright, Designs and Patents Act, 1988.

Printed in Singapore by Tien Wah Press Pte.
ISBN 978-1-84506-587-4

2 4 6 8 10 9 7 5 3 1

Me and My Dad!

Alison Ritchie

illustrated by Alison Edgson

LITTLE TIGER PRESS
London

My dad wakes me up
every morning, like this –
He tickles my nose and
gives me a kiss.

We go out exploring,
there's so much to see.
My dad knows where all
the best secrets will be!

My dad is a giant —
up here so am I!
If I stretch really hard
I can touch the sky.

We find sticky honey,
our favourite snack.
Watch my dad run when the
bees want it back!

My dad twirls me round
and the world whizzes past.
My head gets all dizzy,
I'm spinning so fast!

If loud thunder roars
and the skies turn to grey,
My dad keeps me safe,
till the storm goes away.

When it's raining my dad
plays a staying-dry trick —
To dodge all the raindrops
we have to be quick!

We race to the river
and Dad jumps straight in.
I climb on his back
and we go for a swim.

My dad is so strong,
he can lift anything.
I hope I'm strong too when I'm
grown-up like him.

When I get sleepy,
Dad gives me a hug
And carries me home,
all cosy and snug.

My dad tells me stories
as day turns to night.
We cuddle up close
in the twinkling light.

My dad is the best
daddy bear there could be.
We're together for ever –
my dad and me.